It's Your Turn At Bat

Meet
MARK

Birthday: December 6
  ("Mom's early Christmas gift")
Best friends:
  Brian McDaniel
  Brenda Dubrowski
  My twin brother Michael
    ("Most of the time")
Hobbies:
  Reporting for the
    Woodburn *Gazette*
    ("Ace Sports Editor: that's me!")
Sports:
  Baseball, baseball, and
    more baseball
  Swimming, too
Favorite food (Yum!):
  Chicken tacos
Favorite subjects:
  History
  Lunch
  Math ("Especially computers")
Yuck!:
  Sweet potatoes
  Putting my clothes away
  Emptying the dishwasher

Mark Riley

THE KIDS ON THE BLOCK BOOK SERIES

It's Your Turn At Bat

Featuring Mark Riley

Barbara Aiello and Jeffrey Shulman
Illustrated by Loel Barr

TWENTY-FIRST CENTURY BOOKS
FREDERICK, MARYLAND

Twenty-First Century Books
38 South Market Street
Frederick, Maryland 21701

Printed in the United States of
America

9 8 7 6 5 4 3

Book designed by Robert Hickey

Special Sales:

Library of Congress Cataloging-in-Publication Data

Aiello, Barbara.
    It's your turn at bat: featuring Mark Riley / by Barbara Aiello
and Jeffrey Shulman; illustrated by Loel Barr.
    (The Kids on the Block book series)
    Summary: While reluctantly doing research on sewing machines for a
school report, Mark, a fifth-grader with cerebral palsy, discovers
that the money for his team's baseball jerseys that he was
responsible for is missing, and he finds himself feeling more
friendly towards sewing machines. Includes a question and answer
section about what it's like to have cerebral palsy.
    ISBN 0-941477-02-9
    [1. Cerebral palsy—Fiction.   2. Physically handicapped—Fiction.
3. Baseball—Fiction.]   I. Shulman, Jeffrey, 1951– .   II. Barr,
Loel, ill.   III. Title.   IV. Series: Aiello, Barbara. Kids on the
Block book series.
PZ7.A26924It   1988   88-27525
[Fic]—dc19

To the children who teach us about differences—
and similarities

CHAPTER 1

"Now, people," Mr. Beame said very seriously. He was walking down the aisles and placing our last writing assignment on our desks. He didn't look very happy.

"Now, people," he said again. We all knew that when Mr. Beame began one of his "Now, people" speeches, trouble was in the air.

But trouble wasn't the only thing in the air. From somewhere far away an April breeze, warmed by the sun, had made its way to the new Woodburn School and Community Center— a pleasant reminder that spring was near. And with spring returning, that could only mean one thing: spring training for the Woodburn Wildcats. Baseball was back!

Like a police officer on patrol, Mr. Beame walked around the classroom. "It is clear to me, and I hope to you, that what is needed here is practice—a lot more practice." I knew he didn't mean practice catching fly balls or running the bases, but that's what was on my mind. At least, that's what was on my mind until I saw Mr. Beame reach for the Slime Box.

"Oh, yuk," I said to myself, "not the Slime Box again." I thought I said it to myself, but Mr. Beame gave me one of his "Now, people" looks to go with his "Now, people" speech. Maybe he could read minds as well as writing assignments, I thought. Boy, I hoped not.

It's not really called the Slime Box. That's the name I gave to Mr. Beame's "Surprise Box," a big, pea-green box he uses to hand out writing assignments. Each time we have a writing assignment, Mr. Beame fills the box with ideas. We have to reach in and pull one out, and whatever you get—well, good luck, because that's what you have to write about. And luck is just what I don't have, at least not when it comes to the Slime Box. Last week the topic was "Occupations," and there were some terrific ideas, like "air traffic controller" or "paramedic." I picked "museum curator." See, that's why I call it the Slime Box. Somehow, it always manages to give me the slimiest choices. Somehow, it just knows. "What now?" I wondered, as the Slime Box made its way around the room.

"What's the topic for this week?" asked Brenda in her too sweet voice.

"Leftovers," Mr. Beame answered.

"Leftovers?" Brian asked. "Like Friday-night dinner at my house?"

"Not those kinds of leftovers, Mr. McDaniel. These are all the ideas that no one has picked yet." He gave the Slime Box a shake. "Here are the leftover ideas. Now, we wouldn't want these ideas to feel left out, would we?"

I sighed and sank in my wheelchair. "Great," I said. "I usually get the worst ideas, and now I'm going to get the worst of the worst."

Brian was the first to pick. "Racehorses: How to Train a Winner," he read out loud. "Hey, that's not too bad," Brian said happily.

"Wouldn't you know it?" I mumbled. "Brian probably got the only decent topic."

Brenda was next. "My turn, Mr. Beame?" she asked in her too, too sweet voice. Brenda stuck her hand into the box and swished the little pieces of paper around and around. "Let me see, let me see," she said. She was really taking her time—and everybody else's, too.

"Will you hurry up, already?" I said. Boy, was I impatient. I let off the brakes on the Cruiser—that's my wheelchair—so I could pull up next to Brenda. I knew my topic would be a dud, but I wanted to get this over with. It was bad enough getting a slimy topic without having to wait a hundred years for it.

Finally, Brenda made up her mind. "Your Sports Hero: A Special Kind of Person," she read. She looked kind of sick, like someone who just ate too much dessert. "May I pick again? I don't really like sports, and I certainly don't have a sports hero."

"You will now, Brenda," was Mr. Beame's frosty reply. "You want to play by the rules of the game, don't you?"

"I'll take that topic, Mr. Beame!" I shouted. "I could do a great job. 'Roberto Clemente: My Baseball Hero.' I mean, that assignment was just made for me, the Sports Editor of the Woodburn *Gazette*. I'll trade with Brenda. What does she know about sports anyway? I know all about it!"

"No, thank you," said Brenda, glaring at me. "I can write about this Robert guy just as well as Mr. I Know All About It."

"*Roberto*, not Robert," I said. "He was from Puerto Rico. His name was Roberto." I had to concentrate. It wasn't easy for me to reach into the dark pit of the Slime Box.

I was so mad I was talking to myself. "Brenda Dubrowski writing about Roberto Clemente, ha! And what do I get to write about?" I was prepared for the worst as I read the bad news: "The Sewing Machine: How It Changed Our Lives." I was prepared for the worst, but not for this! "But, Mr. Beame," I complained. "What in the world do I know about sewing machines?"

"Mark Riley, the Sports Editor of the Woodburn *Gazette* also wants to play by the rules of the game, doesn't he?"

I backed up the Cruiser to my desk. "The sewing machine," I said. "I know how it changed my life. It's made me miserable!"

CHAPTER 2

"Can I walk home with you, Mark?" I heard Brenda say.

I was not in a good mood, to say the least. "You walk, I'll ride," I said quickly.

"Oh, you know what I mean."

I knew what she meant, of course. See, I have CP (that's Cerebral Palsy), and I get around in a wheelchair. But not your ordinary, everyday wheelchair. No, sir. This little baby is my souped-up, super-sport, faster-than-a-speeding-bullet Cruiser! It gets me where I'm going, that's for sure.

"I'm sorry, Brenda," I said. I guess it wasn't her fault she picked my Slime Box topic.

"I'm sorry, too," she said. We walked quietly for a little while. I was thinking about baseball, about batting averages and stolen bases and the World Series. I was thinking how good that warm breeze was going to feel in a new Wildcats uniform.

"The Light," I said.

"Say that again," said Brenda. "I didn't get it." Sometimes it's hard for people to understand me because I have CP.

I took a deep breath and spoke slowly. "The Light," I said again. "That was one of Roberto Clemente's nicknames. He was the shining light of the Pittsburgh Pirates from 1955 to 1972."

"You sure know a lot about him."

"My grandfather was a big fan of his. Roberto was born in Carolina, Puerto Rico. When he was a little boy, he and his friends would make their own baseballs and play in vacant lots. You want to know something, Brenda?"

"Sure," she said. I could tell she was getting interested.

"The last time he was up at bat, on September 30, 1972, Roberto got his 3,000th hit. Only ten other men ever had that many hits."

"Why was that his last hit? Did he stop playing?" she asked.

"Well, sort of," I explained. "After the 1972 season there was a terrible earthquake in a place called Mana– . . . a place called Manag– . . . ." I couldn't quite get the words out. You try saying, "Managua, Nicaragua" with CP. Or just try saying it without CP! "Well, anyway, there was a real terrible earthquake. And Roberto was delivering food and clothing and medicine to the people there when the plane he was on crashed. He was killed."

We were both quiet for a little while. There was still just a touch of winter in the air, despite the bright April sunshine.

"He *was* a shining light, wasn't he?" Brenda said.

"Yeah," I said. "You know, I have his autograph. I even have the program from the time he was made a Hall of Famer. His whole life history is in it. I guess you could borrow it for your report."

"That would be great," she said. "Do you have any ideas about the sewing machine?"

"Don't even mention it. I'm trying not to think about it."

"Look, Mark," Brenda suggested, "Why don't you just talk to someone who knows about sewing, someone who's been sewing for a long time?"

"Like who?" I asked. I still wasn't in a very good mood.

"Like—I don't know. But I know there's a sewing machine in the Senior Center. Somebody must use it. Hey, you're a reporter, aren't you? Do some snooping around."

"I am a *sports* reporter," I explained. "Not a sewing-machine reporter. But I guess it couldn't hurt." I was trying to feel enthusiastic, but it wasn't easy.

CHAPTER 3

The Woodburn School and Community Center was a new place this year. "Better than ever," the assistant principal, Mr. Mohammadi, was fond of saying. "The day-care program and the Senior Center have brought new life to this old building. Better than ever, I say."

With Mr. Beame's permission, I wheeled my way to the Senior Center. "And what can I do for you?" asked a friendly voice behind the front desk.

I spoke slowly, breathing deeply. "I'd like to speak to someone who uses the sewing machine here. It's for a writing assignment."

"Oh, you want to talk to the 'Olympic Grandma.' Just hang on a minute, and I'll see what I can do."

"The 'Olympic Grandma,' " I said to myself. "Now what did I get myself into?" I looked around the Center a little bit. There was the sewing machine, all right. It looked like a real old one to me. "Boy, whoever uses this one," I figured, "must be ninety years old. Brenda and her ideas!"

"Hi! I'm Evelyn Rothman. How can I help you?" I wheeled around, and, yes, there stood the "Olympic Grandma." She was old (as old as my grandfather, I guess), but she didn't *seem* old. In fact, she looked like she was ready for spring tryouts for the Woodburn Wildcats. She was wearing a bright blue jogging suit and a headband with the Wildcats logo on it. Not exactly what I expected. I guess I was staring, but I had never seen an "Olympic Grandma" before. "Anything wrong?" she asked.

"Um, no," I said. "Well, I mean, yes, but—" Oh, what a time
to get tongue-tied! I took another deep breath and began to tell
her all about the writing assignment. "I really wanted to write
on sports," I said. "That's my beat, you know."

"Your beat?" she asked.

"Mark Riley," I said, "Sports Editor." And I stuck out my hand.

"Well, how do you do, Mark Riley?" she said, taking my hand. "Evvy Rothman at your service—aerobics instructor and basketball referee. And you can shake on it!" And we did—one sports fan to another. "But, Mark," she continued, "you *did* pick the sewing machine assignment."

"Just unlucky, I guess."

"Unlucky? No way, Mr. Riley. That sewing machine has changed my life, and it changed the lives of lots of other people, too." Mrs. Rothman took a moment to think. "It's made life easier in some ways and harder in others. But for better or worse, the sewing machine is now a part of American history. Unlucky! I dare say, Mark, you may have the best topic of all." I wasn't about to argue with the "Olympic Grandma," even if I still wasn't convinced. "Now," she said, "let's show you how this old thing works."

Mrs. Rothman sat herself at the sewing machine and took out a small piece of green-checkered cloth. "That looks familiar," I said.

"It should," said Mrs. Rothman. "This is the material we used to make the tablecloths for the school cafeteria."

"No kidding? You and the other old"—

"Me," she interrupted, "and the other *senior citizens*. What do you think we do all day—take naps and watch television? Now, come over here. See: this little fork is called the presserfoot. The fabric is gently fed underneath the presserfoot. But the power comes from below, from the treadle," she said, pointing to a metal plate at the base of the sewing machine. "As you feed the fabric here, you pump the treadle like this. And away we go!"

Sure enough, the machine started to whir and made tiny white stitches in the cloth. It reminded me of the stitches in a baseball, and I thought about Roberto Clemente and his friends winding string around and around and around a golf ball and taping together a homemade baseball. I guess the sewing machine *did* change the way baseballs were made. I had never thought about that before. "Okay, Sports Fan," said Mrs. Rothman, bringing me back from Puerto Rico. "Your turn at bat."

"What?" I asked.

"Your turn at bat," she repeated.

"I wish I could," I said. It really looked like fun. "But I don't think my legs will be able to pump the treadle. I have Cerebral Palsy, you see."

"Hmmm" was all she replied. I didn't know what she was "hmmming" about. I was just about to tell her that she didn't have to feel sorry for me—some people do, you know—when she shouted "I've got it!" so loud I nearly did a wheelie in the Cruiser. "You," she said, pointing to me, "out of that contraption,"—

"My Cruiser, you mean."

"Yes, yes, out of that Cruiser and up to the sewing machine, young man. You feed the cloth, I'll pump the pedals—and we'll be cooking with gas!" With the help of a nearby chair, I lifted myself up as far as I could. Mrs. Rothman helped me slide my legs up to the sewing machine.

What a sight. I was sitting in Mrs. Rothman's chair, guiding the checkered cloth through the presserfoot, and there was Mrs. Rothman—flat on her stomach underneath the sewing machine—pumping the treadle with her hands. What a sight!

"Are we cooking, Mark?" she shouted above the noise of the machine.

"We're cooking with gas!" I shouted back.

16

CHAPTER 4

The warm April breeze that floated through Mr. Beame's classroom did not lie: spring was here. The gray winter sky made way for days of brilliant sunshine when everything seemed alive. Spring training days! No one could have seen the storm clouds gathering just beyond the horizon.

Our first game, in fact, was only two days away, and it was an important one. We were scheduled to face the Northwestern Grizzlies, the best team in town. We had never beaten them. We had never even come close.

That day at practice, while I was warming up, I heard a familiar voice in the stands. "Hey, Sports Editor, what position do you play?" It was Mrs. Rothman. I wheeled over to say hello.

"I'm the DH, Mrs. R."

"DH? That's a new one on me," she said.

"DH means 'designated hitter,'" I explained to her. "In the American League, the designated hitter bats for the pitcher. That's my job: to drive in the big runs. Lots of great players have been DH's: Reggie Jackson, Lee May"—

"How about Roberto Clemente?" asked Brenda, who seemed to pop up from behind Mrs. Rothman.

"No. Not Roberto Clemente," I said. "First of all, he played before there were designated hitters. And he played in the National League."

"I know that," Brenda shot back. "He was drafted in 1954 by the Brooklyn Dodgers. He was playing minor league baseball in Montreal."

I was stunned. I was shocked. I was impressed.

"Well, he didn't play in uniforms like those," said Mrs. Rothman before I could think of anything halfway intelligent to say to Brenda. See, Mrs. Rothman was pointing to my fading Wildcats jersey. "Your uniforms are a mess. The letters are all worn off. The colors are all faded. No wonder you can't beat the Northwestern Grizzlies. I always say: you have to look good to play good."

"Don't sweat it, Mrs. R.," I assured her. "Coach Kontos has ordered new jerseys for the team, jerseys with a big, bright-gold wildcat snarling on the front. That should put the fear of Woodburn into those Grizzlies. And I, yours truly, the Woodburn Wildcats team manager, picked the design myself."

Being manager of the Woodburn Wildcats was a lot of responsibility this year. The Wildcats had to raise money for new team jerseys, and guess who was put in charge of the car washes and bake sales and about a million other things? Guess who organized the "PizzaFest" at Polotti's Pizza Palace? I didn't realize it would be so much work. But it was fun, too. Especially when Brenda got soaked at the Saturday car wash. It wasn't my fault, I swear it. The hose just sort of slipped out of my hand. But, boy, was she mad!

"I hope they're not late," Mrs. Rothman cautioned.

I was thinking the same thing myself. I had been bugging Coach Kontos about the jerseys for weeks. I was worried. The whole team was really counting on those jerseys. But I tried not to sound worried.

"I better get back to practice," I said.

"And what about practice on the old you know what?" asked Mrs. Rothman. She meant, of course, the sewing machine. I had been practicing almost every day. I even helped Mrs. Rothman make curtains for the Senior Center. Can you imagine that?

Mark Riley: ace Sports Editor, champion Cruiser driver, DH for the Woodburn Wildcats, and part-time curtain maker.

"What's an 'old you know what'?" Brenda asked.

"Never you mind," I said.

"Well, maybe when you're done practicing the 'old I don't know what,'" Brenda said, "we can talk more about the 1971 World Series between the Pirates and the Baltimore Orioles. Did you know that Roberto Clemente hit .414 with 12 hits and 2 home runs? Now, that was a wonderful World Series."

Great, I thought to myself. Brenda Dubrowski, the baseball expert. She had a lot to learn.

CHAPTER 5

Roberto Clemente's last name means "mild" or "gentle." He was my sports hero, but I was certainly not mild or gentle when I heard about the jerseys. It was the day before our big game.

I was on my way to the Senior Center to interview Mrs. Rothman about what changes the sewing machine had brought to her life. I had already researched how the sewing machine affected the way people worked in America, but I figured Mr. Beame would like the personal angle. The spirit of great journalism: it's in my blood.

I was cruising past the gym when I noticed a light on in Coach Kontos's office. The Coach was sitting at his desk as still as a statue. He didn't even seem to notice me.

"Missing," the Coach said quietly.

"What's that, Coach?" I said. I could hardly hear him.

"It's missing," he said.

"What's missing?" I asked somewhat nervously.

"The money is missing," the Coach explained. His voice was getting louder now.

"What . . . what . . . money is missing?" I said very nervously.

"Our money is missing!" His voice was very loud now. Then he just slumped back into his chair and said in almost a whisper, "Our money is missing. The money for the jerseys is missing."

"Missing? Coach, it can't . . . it can't . . . be missing. I kept it in your bottom drawer. In your bottom drawer, Coach." I wheeled around to the other side of the Coach's big desk. The bottom drawer was open—open and empty. Completely empty.

Suddenly, I felt completely empty, too. I felt like I had just struck out in the bottom of the ninth with bases loaded in the final game of the World Series. "But it has to be here," I shouted.

"It has to be," Coach Kontos said, "but it isn't. It just isn't." He looked at me, and he sounded stern and serious. "Mark," he said. "Try to remember: when was the last time you saw the money?"

I couldn't concentrate on the Coach's question. I began to understand something now. The Coach was asking me what *I* had done with the money.

"Mark?"

"What . . . what . . . are you asking *me* for?" I was almost shouting. "I didn't lose it! I know I didn't lose it." I didn't know what else to say. The money just *had* to be there. "I'll bet someone stole . . . stole it!"

"Now, slow down, Mark. Slow down," Coach Kontos said. "I don't think anyone would want to steal the team's money."

"Sure . . . sure they would!" Now, I *was* shouting. "Maybe somebody from the Grizzlies stole it. They . . . they could have done it, Coach. Or maybe Mr. McFee, the janitor. He could have found it. Or maybe Mr. Beame. He hates baseball. Or maybe Brenda. She was so mad about the car wash. Or maybe"—

"That's just about enough, young man," Coach Kontos interrupted. It was a good thing, too. I was out of breath from trying to think of who might have taken the money. "I don't like to hear people being accused like this. There is no evidence that anyone stole the money, and only you and I have keys to this drawer. The money was probably misplaced. Now, please, try to remember: when was the last time you saw the money?"

"I can't . . . I can't . . . remember. I'm sure I put the money back after the fifth-grade bake sale. I'm sure, Coach." At least, I thought I was sure. I just couldn't think.

"I'm sure you did, Mark. It's not your fault."

"But maybe we can get the jerseys, anyway. We could pay later. I could plan a new car wash and"—

"I'm afraid not. I've already called about it. No money, no jerseys."

"No money, no jerseys," I repeated in a whisper. "What will we do now?"

"Well," he said, "there's really not much we can do, I guess. I'm sorry."

Sorry? I was the one who was sorry. Sorry for Coach Kontos. Sorry for the Wildcats. And sorry for myself. I was especially sorry for myself. I was late for my appointment with Mrs. Rothman, and I was sorry about that, too.

Of course, I told her the whole sad story. "How will I ever explain it to the team? Where could the money be?"

"You're a reporter, Mark." You could tell she was trying to sound hopeful. "So report! Dig into it. Scour the school. Interview anyone who"—

I stopped her before she got too hopeful. "I'm a sports reporter," I explained, "not a missing-team-money reporter. That's a job," I said with a big sigh, "for the police. And I have a pretty good hunch who they'll be looking for."

Mrs. Rothman thought for a minute. "Couldn't we still try to raise the money?" she asked. "There's the PTA. There's Mr. Polotti. I just know he'd help out." She still sounded hopeful. Boy, that was starting to get me angry. Here I was, being as miserable as I knew how, and she was trying to cheer me up. I didn't need cheering up. I needed the money!

"No," I said firmly. "It's too late. The game's tomorrow."

"Well," she said, "we'll just have to figure another way out of this."

"We?" I asked in return.

"You don't think I'm going to let you go into the first big game of the season without being dressed for the occasion? I told you: you have to look good to play good. We'll think of something."

"We'll think of something," I kept repeating to myself. An idea began brewing deep down in my brain. It grew like a summer thunderstorm. You could hear the rumbling warnings growing louder and louder. A brainstorm! There *was* a way out.

Why didn't I think of it before? It was so obvious. "Mrs. R., I've got it! The sewing machine! *You* could sew new jerseys. *You* could save the day!"

"Whoa! Hold on there. I can't sew new jerseys, and I can't save the day. That old sewing machine isn't up to the task. And neither am I. I'm just too busy."

"But . . . but . . . I could help," I interrupted. I was much too excited to take "No" for an answer. "We're a great team! This is just what you've been saying: the sewing machine really can change people's lives. We can do it, Mrs. R. We just have to."

Mrs. Rothman took a long time before answering. I just knew she'd say okay. I just knew it. The only problem was she just didn't say it. "I'd like to be your hero, Mark. I'd really like to come to the rescue. I guess if this were a story, that's exactly what would happen. We'd crank up that machine for one last job, work around the clock to sew new jerseys, and send you out against the Grizzlies looking like the pros on opening day. But this isn't a story. And I don't have a happy ending for you. I'm sorry. Sometimes in real life heroes are hard to find."

I didn't say a word. I just sat there, sulking. I wanted Mrs. Rothman to feel bad. She could do it if she really wanted to. It wasn't fair.

But my sulking didn't change her mind. "It's time to get back to school, Mark. Now, don't give up. We'll find an answer yet. And we *are* a great team."

"Sure *we're* a great team," I said. "Then how come only *one* of us is in big trouble, Mrs. Rothman?"

CHAPTER 6

Team! I just remembered: how was I going to tell the team?

I told them, all right. I told them that afternoon at practice. It should have been a beautiful day. The sun burst through a lingering morning haze, and a gentle breeze puffed away the white wisps of hazy smoke. But I couldn't feel the sun or the breeze. I couldn't feel them inside me. I could only feel dark, angry clouds. Storm clouds that were about to burst.

"Somebody stole the money!" I blurted out as soon as the team had gathered together in the Wildcats dugout.

"How?" Brian asked. It was a simple question. But I didn't have a simple answer.

"I don't know how," I said. "But it's not there, is it?"

"That doesn't mean it was stolen," Jason said.

"Are you saying I took . . . I took it?" I asked angrily.

"No," Brian joined in. "We didn't say you took it."

"So you're saying . . . you're saying I lost it. Is that it?" I wasn't angry anymore: I was mad! There was lightning in those clouds now. It was in my eyes. It was in my voice.

"Well, maybe you misplaced it," Michael suggested. My own brother!

"Team!" I said to myself. "Some team." They sure were teaming up on me.

"And maybe I didn't," I shot back. "Maybe you should have been in charge of the money, if you think it was so easy."

Then everybody started shouting: "You were the team manager! You were responsible!" And the lightning bolts were flashing everywhere.

Just then the Coach's voice broke through the storm: "Let's go, everyone. It's practice time. Show some hustle!"

There was a deep silence. The team slowly started to file out for afternoon practice. No one said a word. But just before he left the dugout, Brian turned around and spoke, I guess, for the whole team: "Thanks a lot, Riley."

CHAPTER 7

By that night, the night before our first game, I wasn't speaking to anyone.

Sometimes I have trouble falling asleep on the night before a big game. But that night was the worst. It was a night full of wild dreams. One dream I had over and over . . .

It was the last game of the 1971 World Series. I was in the first row of Baltimore's Memorial Stadium and just behind the Pittsburgh dugout. There was a sellout crowd rooting for the Orioles. The sun was bright, there was a cool breeze—it was a perfect day for baseball.

"Hot dogs, here! Get your red hots!" It was Mr. Beame. He was selling ballpark franks.

I shouted over the crowd, "One dog, here." You can't go to a ball game and not get a ballpark frank.

Mr. Beame reached into his bin and pulled out . . . and pulled out . . . a paper topic! "Paper topics, here! Get your paper topics," he shouted. And he tossed me a topic—a slimy one at that.

I was about to complain when I noticed an argument on the field. A loud argument. Roberto Clemente and the umpire were shouting at each other. The weird thing was that Roberto didn't have a jersey on. Shoes, pants, hat—but no jersey.

"No jersey, no game!" the umpire was shouting.

"But I didn't lose the money!" Roberto hollered back. "It isn't fair."

The ump was unmoved. "No jersey, no game!"

Roberto stalked off the field. But just before he stepped into the dugout, he looked up at me and said, "Thanks a lot, Riley."

I woke up with a start, breathing hard and sweating. I couldn't fall back asleep. I didn't want to! Not after that dream.

I waited for the morning to come and for whatever the new day would bring. I watched from my upstairs window as a big, orange ball of a sun rose silently from the horizon. There wasn't a cloud in sight. Except in my future, that is. Today was the big game, but for me it was a big disappointment. I looked over my baseball souvenirs. There was the foul ball my Dad caught last year at a Yankees game. Boy, that was a great catch, too. There was the 1966 World Series program. Now, that was an Orioles team to remember.

Somehow, though, it all seemed so sad now. There was my poster of Roberto Clemente. Of all the stuff in my baseball collection, that was my favorite. Roberto was making one of his great leaping catches, both feet high off the ground. I could just see him whipping around and letting that ball fly to pick off the runner racing home from third. "Roberto Clemente: My Baseball Hero." I could have written an "A" paper. On the poster was a quote from Roberto. It was his motto, I guess: "I want to be remembered as a ball player who gave all he had to give."

"All he had to give." I began to think about those words. I remembered that Roberto had his share of tough times. He played when he was hurt. Once, he even played with malaria. Sometimes he struggled at the plate and couldn't get a hit. Sometimes he heard boos from the Pittsburgh fans. But he made it through the tough times. And he gave all he had to give.

I watched the sun turn into a bright yellow circle.

"The Light," I said. I said it to the morning. I said it to whatever the new day would bring.

"What a jerk! What a jerk I've been." I knew what I had done. I guess I knew it all along. I misplaced the money (Where was that money?) and then tried to find someone else to blame. Anyone else to blame. Anyone but Mark Riley, I mean. I looked up at Roberto and knew what he was thinking. "Time for a big-league play, Riley," I said.

Before the game I asked Coach Kontos if I could speak to the team. Team? Well, by this time, it was hardly a team. I don't know what happened to the great Woodburn Wildcats. There they were, sullen and sour. It wasn't just the torn and tattered jerseys. It was something else.

I wheeled into the center of the dugout. I took a deep breath and spoke slowly. "I know how you feel about me," I said, "and I don't blame you. I guess I feel the same way. I want to say, um, just to say . . . I'm sorry. I let you down. I let the team down."

It was quiet and still in the dugout. Like the quiet and still after a big storm.

Brian was the first to speak. "Who cares about a bunch of dumb jerseys, anyway?"

"Yeah," said Michael, "we can beat the Grizzlies without them." That's my brother, I thought.

"Or we could lose to the Grizzlies without them," Jason said. And everybody laughed. For the first time in a long time. It sounded good—and it felt good.

"Well, win or lose," shouted a familiar voice, "it never hurts to look your best."

Imagine my surprise—the whole team's surprise—when Mrs. Rothman charged into the dugout. Imagine my shame after I had been so rude to her.

"That's right," said another familiar voice. "One winning team coming right up," declared Mr. Polotti as he barged into the dugout right on Mrs. Rothman's heels. He was carrying a big laundry bag over his shoulder.

"What's this all about?" Coach Kontos asked.

Mrs. Rothman and Mr. Polotti were grinning from ear to ear. "Show 'em, Polotti," Mrs. R. said. And with that, Mr. Polotti reached into his bag and pulled out . . . and pulled out—

"What is that?" I asked.

"What is this? This," he said, "is an official Polotti delivery boy Woodburn team jersey."

That's what they were, all right—the shirts of Polotti's pizza boys. They were too large ("Extra large," Mr. Polotti explained, "for the team with an extra large heart"), but nobody seemed to mind. On the back was the name "Polotti's" and a fresh-from-the-oven pizza with the works. On the front was a big, green-checkered "W."

"Hey," Brian said, "it looks like the school tablecloths."

"So I had some material left over. Don't complain," Mrs. R. said.

"Leftovers again," laughed Brian. "But I'm not complaining."

No one was complaining. We were all too busy laughing and joking and stuffing extra large pizza jerseys into our pants. We were all too busy being a team again.

"Three cheers for Mrs. R. and Mr. P.," I shouted above the noise. "Hip, hip, hooray!"

It was quite a scene. And when the umpire hollered "Play Ball" and when we took the field for the big game, there wasn't a cloud in the sky.

CHAPTER 8

We lost the big game, but it didn't matter. We celebrated anyway. Pizzas all around—at Polotti's, of course. And the missing money was finally discovered. I found it (I'm sorry to say) in one of the pockets of my backpack. That's where it was all along, I guess. It was not one of my proudest moments, but at least we got to order new team jerseys.

I put the finishing touch on my sewing machine report. I called it "The Tale of the Green-Checkered Wildcat." I was surprised that it wasn't such a bad topic after all. I guess Mr. Beame was surprised, too.

"Well, Mr. Riley," Mr. Beame said, walking down the aisles and placing our writing assignments on our desks. "It looks like the Slime Box didn't let you down this time."

"You mean the Surprise Box, don't you, Mr. Beame?" I said, my face as red as my hair.

"Of course," he said as he handed me an "A" paper. "And, Brenda," Mr. Beame continued, "it looks like you found yourself a sports hero."

"Thanks to the Slime—I mean, the Surprise Box, Mr. Beame." Brenda started to sink in her chair, but Mr. Beame just laughed. "I got an 'A'!" Brenda whispered to me—loud enough for the whole room to hear.

"Can I walk home with you, Brenda?" I asked her after school.

"You ride, I'll walk," she said with a smile.

"So Roberto Clemente came through for you, I guess."

Brenda gave me a funny look. "Who?" she said.

"Roberto. Roberto Clemente. Your sports hero."

"Oh," she said, "he's *your* sports hero. But I found one of my own. See." Brenda handed me her paper. It was titled "Mary Lou Retton: A Big Heart in A Little Package."

"Well, I'll be" was all I could say. "I guess I have a lot to learn, too."

Questions for Mark

Well, that was quite an adventure. I'll bet you have plenty of questions about what it's like to have Cerebral Palsy (CP, for short). That's all right. Here are some questions from kids just like you.

Q. What does it feel like to be sick?

A. First of all, I have to tell you: I'm not sick. When I get a cold, I'm sick. When I get the measles, I'm sick. When I have a math test to study for, I'm sick. But CP? Well, that's just the way I am.

There are all kinds of CP. And there are all kinds of people with CP. People are different, you see, and people with CP are different, too. As I always say, "If you've seen one person with CP, you've seen one person with CP!"

Q. Why are you in a wheelchair?

A. I use a wheelchair because I have Cerebral Palsy. I can't walk like other kids. I have trouble talking, too. But I get around all right, tooling in my wheelchair. You might think it's an ordinary enough wheelchair, but to me it's a souped-up, super-sport, faster-than-a-speeding-bullet "Cruiser." Let me tell you: it's a *bad* machine! Here's a close-up look.

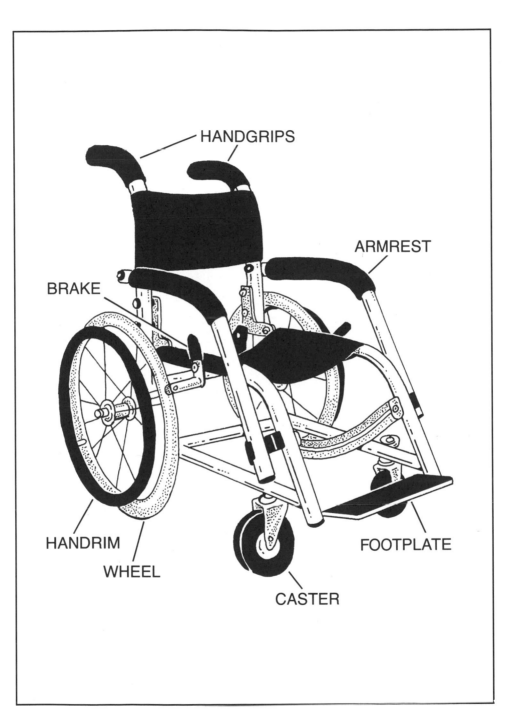

HANDGRIPS

ARMREST

BRAKE

HANDRIM

WHEEL

CASTER

FOOTPLATE

Sorry, no riders allowed.

Q. What is Cerebral Palsy?

A. That's not such an easy question to answer, but I'll try.

CP means that I have a hard time telling my body what to do. You see, the body is a system of communication (like the phone) and movement (like a car). When we want to walk or talk or do just about anything, the brain tells the body what to do. Imagine you just saw a grizzly bear coming toward you. It might be a good idea to put a lot of distance between you and that bear, right? Your brain has the idea: "I'm getting out of here!" So it sends a command through the body's network of nerves to the muscles in the legs. Like, "Don't just stand there. Run!" The legs get the message—and they're off.

But somehow my brain and body aren't communicating. If I want to run, my brain sends out the command, but the muscles in my legs don't hear it. When my brain sends, "Shout it out loud and clear," there must be static on the line because the muscles in my mouth don't do what they're told. Sometimes I wonder, "Who's in charge here, anyway?"

Q. What is it like to have CP?

A. For me, having CP means that I have to work hard to get my muscles to do what I want them to do. Most kids don't think at all about muscles and nerves and that kind of stuff. But I have to concentrate when I want to speak clearly, or when I want to comb my hair, or when I—well, when I want to do just about anything.

40

What's it like to have CP? It's hard, all right. But I try not to let it get me down. If it's hard work to move my muscles, then I work hard at it. I go to a special exercise class for physical therapy. Physical therapy is where I get extra help in using my muscles. A special helper called a physical therapist shows me how to make my muscles stronger and looser, and that makes it easier for me to do the things I want to do. And even though I can't control my leg muscles, it's still important to give them exercise, too. The physical therapist moves my legs to keep the muscles from getting too weak and stiff.

You can try an experiment to get an idea of what it is like to have CP. Put three socks on each of your hands. Now try to button or unbutton your shirt. Not too easy, is it? It takes a lot of practice and patience. And take it from me, it can get pretty frustrating at times, too.

Q. Does having CP mean that you're crippled or handicapped? Does it matter what people call you?

A. It matters a lot. Some words make me feel like I'm weak or helpless or just not as good as everyone else. That's why I don't like to be called "crippled." And that's why I don't like it when people say I'm "confined" to my wheelchair, or "afflicted" with CP, or even when they say I'm "handicapped."

I don't mind it when people say I'm "disabled" because there are some things I'm not able to do. But I like to think about the things I can do—and there are lots of those.

The words that we use to describe other people always matter. Words can hurt just as much as sticks and stones. They can give you the wrong idea about people before you even have a chance to meet them—and that can be a *real* handicap.

Q. But how can you play baseball in a wheelchair?

A. A person in a wheelchair can do lots of things. It just takes the three "C"s: concentration, coordination, and cooperation. Let me tell you what I mean.

When you hit a ball, you have to concentrate. You know, keep your eye on the ball and all that. Well, I have to do that, too, but I also have to concentrate on moving my muscles so that they are working together. When the muscles are working together, that's coordination. And that's a lot easier for most people than it is for me. That's why the other players in my baseball league let me use a special ball and bigger bat when I'm at the plate. So it's easier for me to get a hit. That's what I mean by cooperation—people helping others get in the game!

Q. Can you play other sports?

A. Other sports? Hmmm, let me think.

Well, I can think of a few. How about skiing, badminton, ice skating, archery, weight lifting, horseback riding, bowling, track and field, table tennis, basketball, swimming? And that's just for starters. Did you know that there is a United States Cerebral Palsy Athletic Association? Did you know that there is even a Wheelchair Sports Hall of Fame?

Being a part of the game: that's what it's all about.

Q. But isn't it hard to get around in a wheelchair?

A. You bet it is! But not for the reason you think.

You know why it's hard to get around in a wheelchair? I'll tell you in one word: access. That's right, access. It means "easy to approach or enter." It may not mean much to you, but it means the world to me.

You see, we live in a world that was not made for people in wheelchairs. If you don't believe me, think about what it would be like if you had to be in one for just a day. Could you get around your own house? Could you go to the bathroom? Could you cross the street? Could you go to the movie theater? Could you do a hundred other things? Probably not.

Access means that a place is easy to approach or enter by someone in a wheelchair. It might mean that a ramp has been built next to the stairs or the parking lot, or that a building has a special bathroom, or that there is an elevator to get from floor to floor. Wherever you go, think about how you would get around in a wheelchair.

And look for this sign:

This is the symbol of access. Whenever you see this sign, you know that here is a place where it is easy *for everybody* to approach or enter.

Q. Can you go real fast in your wheelchair?

A. Just try to keep up with me! You run, I'll ride—and we'll see who gets there first.

I used to zoom around the halls in school, too—right past the sign saying "No Running in the Halls!" "Who's running?" I said to myself. That was before the day I came around a corner too fast and nearly crashed into Mr. Beame. Now the sign reads: "No Running *and No Cruising* in the Halls!" Oh, well, that's life in the fast lane.

Q. Why do you talk funny?

A. That's one of the hardest parts of having CP. When you speak, you use many muscles in your mouth and throat. Speaking clearly means there has to be a lot of muscle coordination. When I try to speak, it's very hard to control those muscles, and sometimes my words come out real slow and sound slurred—especially when I get nervous or excited. It's really hard when people just can't understand what you're trying to say or when they think you must be stupid.

Here's something you can try to see what it's like to talk with CP. Put your tongue behind your bottom front teeth, keep it there, and say the "Pledge of Allegiance." Well, how did that sound? Try the same thing with a friend listening. How does it feel to talk in a different way?

Q. Do other people in your family have CP?

A. No. And you can't catch it either. When we were born, my twin brother Michael got a lot of the same things I did, but he didn't get CP.

I'm not sure what causes CP. The doctors say that there are many kinds of CP and many different causes. Somehow, when I was very, very young, the part of my brain that controls the body's muscles was damaged. But it is important to remember that CP is not something you can catch from me. And you can't get it from Michael, either!

Q. Why do you wear a helmet? Do you play football, too?

A. No, I don't play football. And it's not a helmet. It's called "headgear," and I wear it in case I have a seizure. It's kind of hard to explain what a seizure is. The doctors say it means that the messages from my brain to my body are getting all mixed up, and my muscles start to shake real fast and real hard. I could even fall out of my wheelchair. So I wear my headgear just in case. After all, I have to protect my great brains!

Q. Will you get better?

A. That depends on what you mean. If you mean, "Will my CP be cured?" the answer is no. But I can work hard to learn how to control my muscles better and do more and more things. There are some things I will never be able to do, but I'm going to try to do everything I can!

Q. Are you sad that you have CP?

A. Sometimes, I guess. Especially when people tease me, or treat me like I'm sick or like a baby—or like I don't exist at all. But most of the time, I hardly ever think about it. Maybe I'm just used to it. Having CP just seems to be a part of *me*—and now I concentrate on just being the best me I can!

About The Kids on the Block

Founded in 1977 by Barbara Aiello, The Kids on the Block puppet program was formed to introduce young audiences to the topic of children with disabilities. Since then the goals and programs of The Kids on the Block have evolved and broadened to encompass a wide spectrum of individual differences and social concerns.

Barbara Aiello is nationally recognized for her work in special education. The former editor of *Teaching Exceptional Children*, Ms. Aiello has won numerous awards for her work with The Kids on the Block, including the President's Committee on Employment of the Handicapped Distinguished Service Award, the Easter Seal Communications Award for Outstanding Public Service, and the Epilepsy Foundation of America's Outstanding Achievement Award. Her puppets have appeared in all 50 states and throughout the world. In addition, over 1,000 groups in the United States and abroad make The Kids on the Block puppets an effective part of their community programs.

For More Information

The Kids on the Block
9385-C Gerwig Lane
Columbia, Maryland 21046
800-368-KIDS

United Cerebral Palsy Association
(UCPA)
66 E. 34th St.
New York, NY 10016
212-481-6300
800-872-1827

National Information Center for
    Handicapped Children and Youth
7926 Jones Branch Dr.
Suite 1100
McLean, VA 22102
703-893-6061

United States Cerebral Palsy
    Athletic Association
34518 Warren Rd.
Suite 264
Westland, MI 48185
313-425-8961